SELF TALK:
Commonly Uncommon

COMPILERS:

KANAN SHARMA &
DISHA SANGTANI

Spectrum Of Thoughts

AM/56, Basanti Colony, Rourkela, 769012, Odisha

An Affiliate Of FanatiXx

Website :- www.sotpublication.com

ACKNOWLEDGEMENT

First and foremost, we would like to thank the Almighty for the reason we are here today. We also thank every soul who helped us bring this book to fruition.

We wholeheartedly thank the Heads of our team, Srashti Behure and Mayuri Valanju for their invaluable support in completing this mammoth project in record time.

We thank the Spectrum of Thoughts Publication teams, for providing all our budding writers including myself, with this creative platform.
We thank all the co-authors forging us at every step their patience and faith in us during the making of this Anthology.

We would like to give our wholehearted thanks to the Designer, Sagar Samal for creating such an attractive cover page. We also thank the books' Interior Designers, Neharika Bhatia and Mayuri Valanju for lending their aesthetic expertise to the pages of the book.

DISCLAIMER

This Anthology is a melody of memories. The writers have beautifully described their every emotion through their write-ups and they have given their words that the write-ups are free from plagiarism.

So, if any plagiarism is detected in the book neither the publishing house nor the compiler will be responsible.

Co-Authors Onboard

1. Vikram Brahma
2. Tiana Motiani
3. D.V.Rathore
4. Diksha Kumawat
5. Niharika Kaushik
6. Aadarshini Singh
7. Neha Kaushik
8. Somya Nandwani
9. Radhika Dua
10. Jyotika
11. Sumedha Vats
12. Vidya Hariharan
13. Shalini Das
14. Dhyana Buch
15. Nilesh Sangtani
16. Unnati Chandwani
17. Hitika Awtani
18. Bhumika Parmar

Kanan Sharma

(Compiler)

Kanan Sharma is a student and has immense interest in poem composition. She published her book titled 'Loyalty: The Eminent Virtue' in the year 2018. Several of her compositions have also been published in the esteemed newspaper 'Times of India' Student Edition. She is always keen on reaching the masses through her verses and bringing about a positive change in the society.

Disha Sangtani

(Compiler)

Disha Sangtani is from Rajkot. She is an artist, a poetess, and a writer who has a dream of becoming an author one day and a renowned artist.

Dowry

It is a girl's fate
To live in the world of hate
No, he is not her supporter
Who? Her life-mate
Love is not for her
For which she always awaits

She is like a prisoner
Who cannot cross the closed gates.
Her life is enclosed
Within the four walls
She is fiddled like the dolls.
She is not known
To the world
Across the closed cage

Dowry is not a gift
It is a symbol of rift
Breaking relations, blood relations
It is not known, what will happen the next
All this is in a girl's life text

No one can change
And cannot range
The tears hidden in her eyes
Hope for someone
To tie her up
In the world of smiles

Vikram Brahma

Vikram Brahma is a full-time writer and digitalpreneur who loves to work from home. He loves to start his work as early as 7:30 am. He is the author of multiple books. Apart from writing serious content, he has a great interest and love in writing books for children. He is also a biker by heart and loves to observe others and learn from them.

Youth - The Real Power Of The Nation

Hello friends, one day in my mind came a story and I am writing this keeping today's youth in mind. This is a story of two close friends and about the progress, they made in life. Parag and Yashwant are childhood best friends. They are studying in the same college and have decided to work in the same company. As per Parag, they should opt for marketing as their specialization and then search for a job in the marketing companies. Both are good students and know how to compete well in the examination. In the final year as expected both passed with flying colours. Once they are out of college they used their networking skill and managed to get jobs in the same company. Now they shifted their base in Delhi for their career growth. Since they are new in the industry they started their career from the bottom of the pyramid. But since they are engaged in the job they are happy and even their parents are also happy. Every day they are learning new things and enjoying their time working and learning. After three months both received permanent employee offer letters. From a trainee, they got promoted as executives. Now they are allowed to work on bigger assignments and projects. They spend the next two years learning more about their company and brands. Now they have understood that to become a good marketer one has to become a good observer of people and their life. Again after two more years they

got promoted and became senior project executives and have more authority to work independently.

We have been reading about their success and we should feel proud about their growth in life. They are the new generation of youth, who are highly talented and practical in life. They are the real power of the nation. If today's youth think and act like them then our country can progress much faster. Because of their job requirement sometimes they have to travel to nearby cities. They have to meet new people, customers and do marketing research for new ideas and products. Both are earning well and living a comfortable life.

Now their parents have decided that they should get married and invite their close friends to their marriage reception. Out of two, it was Parag who got married first.

Since Yashwant is his best friend he helped him immensely. He made sure that things are arranged as per Parag's demand and requirements.

Within the next two years, both got promoted as managers but they were given different brands to work on. It is a big achievement for them that within five to six years they became managers and started managing teams independently. Both have decided to purchase a home in North Delhi and for this purpose, they have discussed their matter with one builder. Luckily, they have arranged enough money for themselves. Apart from this, their parents have also decided to shift their base to Delhi and would like to live with them. Now they all are living like a joint family in the same apartment.

If you will observe their life closely you will notice many differences in their approach towards life and their career. If you want to become successful in life you will

have to apply your habits in life. First of all, you might have noticed that they were sincere students in their college and passed with bright colours. Before leaving college they have already decided their field of specialization and made good networking so they can get the jobs. They worked smart and learned things fast and within six years they could become managers. Their story may look normal but if you observe them closely they look extraordinary. You see for their job they left their town and shifted their base to Delhi and later they purchased a home. This is a big achievement in itself.

Now we are going to learn about the major qualities to become a successful youth. Today's world needs dynamic youth who can take care of themselves and also progress in life. We have to remember that as the population of this world is increasing, resources are sinking and if we will not act swiftly one will lose the opportunity.

Think About Your Future

One of the biggest mistakes today's youth do is they take the future for granted. They have no goals and haven't decided about their career and life. We have to understand that the main purpose of education is to help us identify our life's goals. We have to learn to think about our future. Once you reach the 12th standard your sole purpose for coming 4-6 years should be to prepare yourself for a job in a particular domain. You have to become specialized and have to know as much as you can. In today's time, there are many old jobs which became obsolete and many new jobs have appeared like digital marketing, AI, Coding & robotics. One has to prepare oneself for these kinds of new jobs. Remember with time many things may change. So, one has to prepare himself/herself for the future.

Observe And Learn New Things

Remember whatever profession you will join in the future you will have to continuously learn new things. There was a time when people have no idea about computer literacy and many people ignored it completely. Those who ignored it realized its importance
later when they have to progress in their career. Today having basic knowledge of computer is compulsory. At least one should know how to use MS Office, email, and
basic internet. In the same way, Yashwant and Parag kept themselves relevant with time and kept on learning new things about their job.

Search For A Good Mentor

In life many times having a strong mentor is important. We go to a particular school and college to learn from teachers. In the same way, when we join some company we should follow instructions from a particular senior. I have observed that if your mentor is good then you can easily progress in your career. A good mentor will teach and guide you in every step of your career. Why should we take instructions from a mentor? Well, they are the ones who have gone through the entire process in their career and know the ups and downs of an executive's career. Whether you want to become a sportsman or want to join a company having a good mentor in your life is important.

Work On Your Basic Soft Skills

There are two kinds of skills. One is hard skills and another is soft skills. Hard skills are technical skills that help you get a job. On the other hand, soft skills help you in retaining the job. For example, skills like reading, speaking, writing, eye contact, problem-solving; teamwork, leadership, interpersonal, etc. are good examples of soft skills. These skills help you manage your daily task smoothly. If you want to progress in your career and life then you should learn and use these skills. They are easy to learn and implement in life but you have to practice them on regular basis. These skills help you progress in life and your career. I have seen and observed that if you are good at these skills then you can easily communicate your point of view with colleagues, seniors,
and juniors. Remember these skills will help you in retaining the job so focus on them
too.

Have A Plan And Identify Life's Goal

If you want to become successful, then you need a plan regarding your life's goal. If you check the success story of Yashwant and Parag you will notice that they have started from the bottom of the pyramid. But they kept on learning things and within six years they managed to become successful managers in their respective organizations. They even managed to purchase a home in Delhi and even got married. Successful people always plan for their future. Just like a company thinks and plans for the future; in the same way, we have to learn to think about the future. There are no alternative ways to become successful. Plan, hustle, and make changes in your life. Remember life's goal will give you direction.

Get Organized And Disciplined

What is the number one secret of the success of many athletes in the world? Why they can achieve their goals and targets? If you will ask this question to any successful player he/she will say – it's because of a well-organized plan and discipline. Yes, discipline in life can give you an edge over others. A person who is disciplined in life can achieve great heights. Discipline doesn't apply only to athletes; it does apply to businessmen, teachers, entrepreneurs, military persons, and every other individual. Growth and progress in life are possible only if you follow some set of rules on daily basis. Successful people are well organized and have to build systems with dedication. As youth make sure you also build your set of rules and systems. This can change your life slowly but surely.

Know Your Strength And Weakness

There is a system which is known as SWOT analysis. Where S stands for strengths, W stands for Weaknesses, O stands for opportunities and T stands for threats. In simple words, it is a method for identifying and analysing internal strengths and weaknesses and external opportunities and threats. As an individual one should know his/her strengths and weaknesses and should work on them. For example, suppose you are weak in communication and language then you should work on improving your communication. And if you are good at calculation, mathematics, and physics then you should search for such jobs where you can use your talent perfectly. Yes, as an individual and youth you should know about this. There are vast opportunities related to jobs and careers but you should first introspect yourself. If you will get a job according to your skills and interests you can progress faster in that career. We have shared seven important qualities to become a dynamic youth. Now take a notebook and write down about them one-by-one. Spend some quality time and write in detail as much as possible. Once you will complete this exercise you will get to know many things about yourself. You have to be smart enough in searching for your job or work. As you will spend the next 25-30 years working, therefore, you shouldn't take it lightly. Remember if you will take one wrong decision in life it will have great repercussions in the later stage of your life. It is also true that people learn by doing mistakes. But, if you plan it will give you some edge over others. So, as an author, my honest advice will be that you should prepare yourself well for the future. Just like today's youth want better facilities and structure and in the same way parents, teachers, society and organizations want better-organized youths. They want them to behave well and highly educated and be ready for the industry. As per the survey, many companies have admitted that the college curriculum is not as per industry standards. So, students have to take additional courses to learn about new things that are in demand in the market. For example, when I started working in the year 2004, I knew nothing about digital marketing and its related field. But today this is one of the most demanding careers for today's youth. Nowadays everybody is interested in becoming a content writer, YouTuber, Facebook ad expert, funnel expert, social media content creator, SEO expert, or blogger. Do you know there are many ways through which you can make money if you know how to use digital marketing in the right way? In fact, after leaving my job in 2019 I opted for digital marketing techniques

especially content writing, and was able to make my first $1000. Yes, it takes time to build your online presence and authority. But once that builds you can have a better portfolio and opportunity.

I hope the ideas shared in this book will be beneficial for you especially for youth.

Remember you need to keep your spark, that innocent magic alive. When I say spark it is the beauty, your smile, your eagerness to learn new things and doing better than yesterday. Recently, the world was hit by a pandemic and we all have suffered in our life. Millions have died and the world came to a standstill. Now, people have realized the importance of hygiene and cleanliness. Because of these changes suddenly fuel and food prices went high. And now people have no option but to accept the new rules of the market.

As a youth, we have to understand many things and work accordingly. You have to understand why some youth progress in life and others struggle. If you want to

become successful youth then you have to prepare yourself in advance. Sometimes no one is going to come to your rescue. For example, during the pandemic, many people lost their day job and many small size companies shut their operations. While writing this piece of content I have read in the newspaper that a big organization like Ford is going to stop manufacturing cars in India. They are going to stop manufacturing vehicles in their Gujarat and Chennai plants. It has been said that they have suffered around $2 billion losses in India and due to this and other reasons; they will like to wind down their operations. Now, for a moment think about those workers and executives where they will go, and how they will survive.

Well, I shared this difficult scenario with you because I wanted to tell you that sometimes conditions and situations will change suddenly. Whether they will shut their complete operation or not we will come to know by end of 2022. That's why as a youth you have to keep yourself updated and be ready for the change. Now I have one question for you. As a dynamic youth can you give some solutions for such a scenario?

As a writer when I hear such news I remember my old days because as an executive I have witnessed such a situation two times in my life. I clearly remember I used to work for Motorola as a third-party employee and when they decided to close their operation we were asked to leave the company. Same thing I have witnessed in one advertising agency too. But, I was lucky enough that I left the agency before they stopped their operation. These situations can happen with anyone and as per my limited knowledge; I know that the financial situation of the company plays a major role. Many companies in India and the world are running in losses. That's why you have to make sure to check the company's financial stability before joining the organization. There is no guarantee that big organization means they are running profitably.

Final Words

Before I end this, I also like to share that there are many ways through which one can become a smart and active person. You only have to learn things as you grow in life.

Learning is a continuous process and one can keep on growing if he/she will keep on learning. I hope you remember when you were young you used to learn a, b, c and as you grew a little bigger you started learning about vowels and sentences and then how to read paragraphs. Later when you joined college you opted for specialization and kept on learning. Then you joined a company and again you kept on learning new things. I hope you remember we started this chapter with the examples of two best friends. We saw their growth and improvements in life and career. How they worked hard and reached the managerial level. Got married and even purchased a home for them. They even left their hometown and settled in

Delhi with their parents. And it took them almost five to six years. Remember getting success is a long process. We have to learn to adapt to the situation.

Finally, remember to enjoy life and time as you learn new things. There is no fun getting a promotion when your back is paining or you have lost your mobile. There is time for everything. Don't compare yourself with others. Your time will come but be sure that you will be ready to grab the opportunity. Difficult situations will play their part, so be strong and flexible and always hope for the best. With these words, I like to end this chapter and I hope you have gained some meaningful insights about life and for your career. Remember as a youth, you are the real power of the nation. I wish you all great success and amazing life ahead.

Tiana Motiani

Tiana Motiani is a budding writer of class 4th from Rajkot whose dream is to become a renowned author of a best-selling book. She writes from the core of her soul and believes that poetry is a deep thought.

Weather

Weather,

Is just like my brother

Weather's mood changes every time

But it doesn't do crimes

First comes the weather cold

Which never gets old

Then comes the weather hot

In that you won't like it in your cot

Third is rainy

In this weather I become a baby

These weathers repeat again

You may ask when?

Heroes of COVID-19

Everyday somewhere in the world

Another unsung hero is born

Someone who is willing

To lay his life on the line

To save another creature

On this planet of ours

Like the policemen guarding the streets

Telling everyone to stay home, safe and sweet

Doctors saving lives

Without a thought of their wives

Nurses helping patients to thrive

To get rid of those negative vibes

Can't forget the cleaners

Cleaning the bins and trash

Keeping the world clean in a flash

Thanking them is not enough

Being on their side

Is not tough

Let's fight this hard

By being their part

Staying home apart

STAY HOME STAY SAFE

Wonderful World

This is a pleasure

In the pathless woods

It's heavenly

In the mountains

There is society where no one intrudes

By the deep sea and music in its roar

Time spent amongst trees

Is never wasted time

Land really

Is the best art

The poetry of earth

Is never dead

D. V. Rathore

D. V. Rathore is a dynamic, versatile and very talented poet, working as a class-1 Officer in Govt. of Haryana. He is B.Tech., MBA(HR), PGD in industrial safety management, PGD in HRM, Diploma in Management. He has written around 300 poems on various issues like depression, relationships, motivation, love, etc. He also has a very popular YouTube channel named 'Motivation by DVR'. He is emotionally attached with nature and artists and is passionate about plants and beautiful flowers. Singing, dancing and playing badminton are other hobbies. He always aims to do something special and unique.

मौन

हूँ चुपचाप सा बेचैन सा, क्यूं मौन हूँ मैं,
किसी की याद में खोया हुआ, कौन हूँ मैं?
हूँ बेचैन सा खोया हुआ सा रहता हूँ,
कहना होता है कुछ और, और कुछ कहता हूँ,
जाना होता है कहीं ओर, कहीं चला जाता हूँ,
महफिल में भी एक पल चैन, अब नहीं पाता हूँ,
कभी जो थे परेशान हरकतों से मेरी,
उनके वास्ते खामोश सा एक फोन हूँ मैं,
किसी की याद में खोया हुआ सा, कौन हूँ मैं?

गुजरती सामने से, खुश यूँ ही हो जाता हूँ,
दोबारा कब दिखेगी, सोचने लग जाता हूँ,
कितना देख लूँ फिर भी ये मन नहीं भरता,
सिवाए सोचने के, और कुछ नहीं करता,
बंधा हूँ बंधनों से शांत स एक गौन हूँ मैं,
किसी की याद में खोया हुआ सा, कौन हूँ मैं?

मुझे शक है उसे इस बात की खबर होगी,
अगर होगा पता तो भी कहाँ कद्र होगी,
कभी मिलती है तो नज़रें इनायत होती है,
अगर हँसती है तो मानो कयामत होती है,
बिना उसके हूँ आधा सा, अधूरा पौन हूँ मैं,
किसी की याद में खोया हुआ सा , कौन हूँ मैं?
हूँ चुपचाप सा बेचैन सा, क्यूँ मौन हूँ मैं?
किसी की याद में खोया हुआ सा, कौन हूँ मैं?

जुनून

जब तलक शरीर में रक्त का प्रवाह है,
कर्ण से ध्वनियाँ सुन रही है जब तलक,
जब तलक स्वास ये, मुझमें प्राण भर रही,
दृष्टि से निहार पा रहा हूँ मैं जब तलक,
तब तलक मुझे तेरे इश्क का जुनून है ,
तब तलक मुझे तेरे इश्क का जुनून है।

जब तलक फिजाओं में प्रभात ये बह रही,
नीर से भरी हुई, ये धरा है जब तलक,
जब तलक हयात में, रूह काम कर रही,
सूर्य की प्रभाएं ये, बिखर रही है जब तलक,
तब तलक मुझे तेरे इश्क का जुनून है,
तब तलक मुझे तेरे इश्क का जुनून है।

जब तलक ये आसमां, सितारों से व्याप्त है,
शरीर में सांस की, फुहार है ये जब तलक,
जब तलक जहान के, फलों में ये मिठास है,
दिल के आशियाने में, धड़कने हैं जब तलक,
तब तलक मुझे तेरे इश्क का जुनून है,
तब तलक मुझे तेरे इश्क का जुनून है।

हैलमेट

सूट बूट और चश्मा पहन कर,
जैसे ही मैं घर से निकला,
बिन हैलमेट के टशन बड़ा था,
चौराहे पर टायर फिसला।

मैं गिरा जोर से बीच सड़क पर,
फट गए कपड़े, चश्मा टूटा,
दिखने लगे यमराज मुझे तब,
बाइक टूटी सिर भी फूटा।

शायद मुझसे समय था रूठा,
बीच सड़क पर पड़ा था बेसुध,
फट गए कपड़े, चश्मा टूटा,
फट गए कपड़े, चश्मा टूटा।

याद आई मुझे मेरी छोटी गुड़िया,
जिसने मुझको टोका था,
हैलमेट भूल गये हो पापा,
उसने मुझको रोका था।
कितनी फिक्र थी उसको मेरी,
पर मैंने उसकी नहीं मानी,
बिन मेरे क्या उसका होगा,
इतनी बात भी अब जानी।

हाथ पकड़ रोका था बेटी ने,
पर मैंने कहा कि उसकी मानी,
मैं ही सही हूँ बस यही सोच कर,

कर गया मैं अपनी मनमानी।

अब हाथ जोड़कर माफ़ी माँगू,
बेटी मैं शर्मिंदा हूँ,
बीच सड़क पर पड़ा हूँ बेसुध,
शायद नहीं मैं जिंदा हूं।
पहन लेता हैलमेट जो सिर पर,
इतना टशन दिखाता ना,
होता अब संग अपनों के,
इतना दूर मैं जाता ना।
सुन लेता अपनों की अगर मैं,
अब इतना पछताता ना,
अब इतना पछताता ना।
सबसे पूछूँ बस यही प्रश्न मैं,
बिन हैलमेट यूँ टशन दिखाकर,
क्या मिलता है खोकर अपनो को,
क्या मिलता है उन्हें रुलाकर?

Diksha Kumawat

Diksha Kumawat is an UG student from Chittorgarh, Rajasthan. Being a teenager she started writing her thoughts and started putting them together and they turned out really amazing. A platform like spectrum of thoughts gave her the debut to this writing society. She believes in writing in simple language which everyone can relate to easily. She doesn't really have much friends but a very trustworthy diary, which gives her strength whenever she is in need.

A Dream

I was flying,

on the road,

as if it was a trampoline.

I broke the signal,

no one cared,

as if cops were mingle.

Peachy pink sky,

with dragon flies around,

and the weather was dry.

Kites were flying,

this was first time,

I wasn't crying.

I love to stay,

only there,

as there were no prays.

I was dancing in the streets,

unafraid of anyone,

as I was fearless.

I hate the world,

where I live,

as it is so cruel.

But will never find the one,

of my imagination.

Within Me

Settle down under the white blanket,

with no projects.

Something like cotton was gliding,

with no planning.

Thoughts were on vacation,

inner peace was in motion.

Disturbance was ignored,

as I wasn't bored.

Everything was in the moment,

but the body was in no movement.

Sun was setting,

and the mood was litting.

All the tiredness went away,

when the scene was straight away.

You Never Knew

Far far away from my reach,

but close to my heart.

Unaware of your feelings,

but mine are over falling.

You might not know,

cause you were never told. No?

As you speak,

I literally lose the silence.

But you remain unnoticed,

cause ya! I control my senses to the best.

Your thoughts leave me smiling,

and that's true I'm not lying.

NOTE: Confessing this to him was my wildest fantasy

ever. Hope he'll read this one someday.

An Evening with Favourite

Sitting with my fav **briend***,

beside the breezing door,

his bullshits, my laughter,

maa screaming, cause mosquito enters,

bread-jam in the hands,

little droplets on the pants,

there comes a sparrow,

which blows our curbs,

we run behind it,

but for obvious, it flies,

and we giggle.

***Briend=Brother + Friend**

Niharika Kaushik

Niharika Kaushik is a Bachelor in Commerce and is about to get her Master's degree in the same. She likes to paint, dance, write and talk to herself. She is her own cheerleader. She is a Sorcery Enthusiast and deeply desires to be able to practice 'Magic'.

Unleashing my Muse

You can't do, they said.

But I had different plans instead.

When they daunted my abilities,

I told myself to show them the possibilities.

When they laughed, questioned,

I smiled as I knew where I was destined.

There were days when I wanted to sleep a little longer,

But I told myself to grow stronger.

Movies, parties and friends

But there was no time to spend.

Some days I wanted to ditch the rules,

But I told myself not to find an excuse.

My weary eyes sought rest,

But I told myself this is the only test.

When my body started giving up,

I relaxed and came back with a higher jump.

Brawling with myself,

I had become my biggest critique,

And improvement became my only technique.

Finally, as I stood for screening,

I recalled the prickling.

It shredded the anxiety,

And I gained the authority.

Today, I stand at a monumental height,

Looking down at their plight.

I told myself not to return the same,

'Cause not everyone can play the game.

An Abstract Battle

Torn between my shoulder angel and devil,

I found the misery reaching another level.

The joust saw no end,

As they craved my consent.

The debate was ad-rem,

But I couldn't conclude them.

The fallen told me to avenge,

The holy told me to prevent.

The red wings ignited me with anger,

The ivory wrapped me to make the flames surrender.

I opened my eyes to the echoes of the mean.

And the world seemed so obscene.

Walking through the flagrant streets,

I witnessed a debased fleet.

Conspiracy, treachery and rapacity had engulfed the city,

Which spared not even the witty.

I sat in the middle,

And cared so little.

The wrath surfaced itself as flames,

And I had the world to blame.

The fallen fuelled the fire,

And guarded me to acquire.

Soon I found myself tied in a silvery rope,

I strangled as it was difficult to cope.

The angelic tried to tame,

But I was adamant with my claim.

Seeing my resolute,

She filed no suit.

As she walked away,

I saw myself decay.

I realized I had chosen the fallacious,

So I stepped towards the gracious.

The darkness tried to hold,

It wasn't me, I told.

The murk scattered,

And the misery shattered.

I knew where I have to walk,

So I gave a knock.

The door opened,

And a unique perspective creeped in.

There was peace and harmony,

And no guilt within.

The riddle solved,

As I evolved.

Enlightened Self

Life is unfair, I thought.

I give a lot and get so short.

The voice inside me overheard,

And said, wait a minute young bird.

Has the sun ever asked for his claim,

Or was reward his aim?

Did the rain cease to shower,

If it wasn't welcomed with a flower?

Will the wind break the flow,

If it doesn't get a big awe?

No, I answered.

It said, then why is life cursed?

The rationale behind life is service,

Then how can be it biased?

Shed the expectations,

And cherish the explorations.

How? I asked,

Master the oneness,

Then you'll feel the fullness.

Lose your identity,

And get lost into nonentity.

The inner self knows it all,

Then why does one think so small.

I smiled and halted the cursing,

Following the Enlightenment,

My life took a turning.

The meaning of life is established,

And that's all I had wished.

An Enchanted Thought

What if I had magic?

It would be ecstatic.

Walking in the air,

I will leave behind a flowery fair.

Diving into the tributary,

I thought, I will meet the Oceanic dignitary.

Ascending the highest peak,

I would not feel weak.

Jumping off the cliff,

I will land so swift.

I thought, 'Is it all I want?'

Why not fix the broken,

And sense the unspoken.

Unfurl tranquillity,

And Corroborate stability.

Aadarshini Singh

A student and an ambitious poet at Spectrum of Thoughts, **Aadarshini Singh** has an inclination towards literature. The aim of her compositions is to enthrall the reader in a fleeting reverie, an extract of their veiled thoughts and feelings. She has authored numerous poems on Wattpad, accompanying her very own blog, "Uncovering Realizations".

The Otherworldly Thought

Somewhere among the remote meadows of the mind,
along the dampened ardours and words I've been concealing,
lies this esoteric emotion struggling to be heard,
being suppressed and silenced, an arcane feeling.
It screams, shrieks, squeals and squawks,
it bellows its thoughts till it desires,
It strangles my soul and drowns my heart,
and to my wings, it sets fire.
It pulls out the buried thoughts from the depths,
presents the pretermitted echoes I never wanted to remember.
The knowledge of my frame being virescent doesn't suffice,
for it exhibits that others' vicinity glimmers like ember.

The Ragged Rubber

Fatigu'd feet, heading bedward,
the erstwhile grubble for what thee desire.
And the wand'ring soul with ragg'd rubb'r,
yond is engluf'd into the fire.

where the glimm'r in thy eyes hid's,
wherefore thee behold the flam's?
if't be true thee art unaware of rules,
wherefore thee play the gam's?

The lady singeth thy lyrics,
h'r feet danceth to thy song.
thy eyes followeth h'r steps,
but thy heart burneth as if't be so wrong.

The audience clapeth and chuckle,
thee whisp'r as people stareth in awe.
And then thy lonely heart
keeps reminding thee of thy flaw.

To Love A Delusion

Why did I see it coming,
why did I have to know,
maybe you knew me better,
but decided to keep the show.
Is it too late to ask why,
where did it all go wrong?
All I have is a distant memory,
why did I know it all along.
But I fell in love with an idea
of how it was supposed to be
the delusion was so comforting,
I lost touch of reality
but as I see the fine print
and the feel the weight of the words in it,
the dream shattered, thoughts scattered,
heart tattered, I couldn't commit
But it was an idea, wasn't it?
Just a rough plan,
and if it already ended,
why am I back to where it began.
I'm sealing the broken pieces,
knitting the rags again,
I gave it all to just an idea
just an outline, simple and plain.

Breathe

The wind's soft kiss and the quilt of gold,
sombre streets serving stories untold.
From the fragments of hope that keep peeking from the sky
to the doleful demeanour of dreams that die.
The captivity of hesitancy that never vacates the mind,
and the lives once lived, all left behind.
When the sensitive skin hugs the harsh gravel,
morose manners; mundane mysteries to unravel,
left with a lugubrious look on the brow,
didn't feel alive but lived somehow.
But when the clock stopped ticking, offered a long-awaited pause,
to breathe, to feel, to smile and to love, without a cause.
For he truly learnt to breathe, just when the moment stopped,
but as the minutes went by, his smile soon dropped.
Flattened his aureate attire and carried the expensive leather.
Encircled by inky fluff, weathering the blustery weather.
Before twisting the door knob, tendered a last thought to the dry heather.

The Dark Heaven

The stories have all told us that beneath darkness lie those shadows,

and that cold hand, the touch of which can destroy...

They go on, that the light brings warmth, a joy,

a safe captivity to free us from our fears and sins...

But they don't tell you that darkness has its own kingdom,

and many living things dwell in it...

They don't tell you that only the warmth inside assuages the dark,

nor will they mention how the night has its own laws.

They won't say that hell is burning bright, and that

angels dwell in silent nights...

They will only say that the battles are of angles and demons,

and that of light and dark.

And that only two elements have ever existed to be known,

and of which victory is defined by only one...

They are scared to agree that in darkness thrived the stars,

and how it comforts us to sleep...

And those who are afraid of the night,

are unaware of the day's mischief and crimes.

And how the anonymity of the darkness has the power to grow roses,

that sunshine can burn groups of forests.

And these stories don't ever mention how the real fights

are those between the dark heaven of goodness and the sinful daylight...

These are the battles that we see every day, and mistake them

for the ones in our fairylands...

A Home

Minding my business and I was walking alone,
trying to find this place they call home,
I step on the wet grass, stumble upon some stones,
the street lights pity me as they watch me roam.
Until I see a path I have never seen before,
the rain tickles my shoulder, drenches my core,
my soul begs for shelter, others say I should explore.
Maybe I'll reach there, maybe I won't have to try anymore.
Deep down, I'm not sure, but as I watch the clouds in grey,
I know I need no diversions, that's what my thoughts say,
as the wind blows by, the warm breeze of May,
it thaws my heart, the sunset ends the day.
the darker skies approach, I'm still on the street,
lit by shooting stars, sore are my feet.
Just as I'm about to retreat,
I turn around, maybe finally accept defeat?
Until a familiar voice is heard, the melody, silver-toned
the comfort it brought; my tangled dreams were all combed.
Suddenly all of this didn't matter, I forgot the streets I once roamed,
for in each note's euphony, I found my home.

Neha Kaushik

Neha Kaushik is a Double Masters in Gender and English Literature. An old-school girl with a modern outlook towards the world. Loves rain and petrichor. Likes to sing, write, read and shop. She wants the world to be a better place and the planet to be happier. She creates memories with places.

Reminiscing

Driving past the flyover
hovered a pool of memories
Of all the timeless ceremonies
And all the beautiful bedtime stories
The mother of my mother's mother
nested among the scenic colors
Amidst the nature trail and the river
She dwelled
The rustic landscape gave her
an innate earthy smell
Craving to find her eternal existence
My heart fought with every logical resistance
For my mind knew she was nowhere to be found

but heart asked to just take a stroll around
She might be found sitting fore the temple
Asking the Gods for the prosperities ample
She must be nearby her closet
Searching sweet eatables for me through
each vault and every pocket
A voice inside my head asked to go inside and

look for her
As the little street was still engulfed with the

fragrance from the same incense burner

My heart thumped as I stepped out of my car
The echoes of the place coerced me to look for the lost star
The mind wanted me to turn and go
But the heart asked to trace her and follow.
The mind warned, "It would be useless."

I, however, did not want to risk the precious.
The heart encouraged me to seek for some imprints
I found no image, no footprints
The tribulations led me

to the waters of Yamuna flowing nearby
The heart and the mind hopelessly

waited for my reply
There began a serious conversation between the three
The mind, the heart and the soul
The two wanted to break free, but
The Soul asked, "Behold!"
If only you would sit and please
She vivres in the sweet vines and fragrant breeze
You may not see those gleamy pair of eyes

But, she looks at you from above the sunrise
Her silhouette might not appear,
But, she will be present in your moments of joy and cheer.

The three came to sound in unison as they agreed
Grandparents are to be loved and reminisced
For this place was always hers and always will be.

The Tongue of Grit

Losing an argument, I thought
What if my gut could speak through tongue
As there were numerous wounds and scars
Through which my heart was severely stung
I wished for an answer, but
Couldn't utter a word
Though eyes were full,
Morals not stirred
Goddess of wit
Smiled at me, pitied me
Gave voice to my gut
So I could speak fearlessly
They hurled their questions, piercing taunts
I paused, gave a little thought
Delivered them with multitude of haunts
They challenged my gender
Questioned my values
I proved my calibre
It cleared the curfew
In every social gathering or affairs
Their fingers pointed towards me
I wore my antiglares
All I could see was their burning envy

All hurtful comments they poured
I smashed them with my tongue of sword
The Goddess congratulated
As I didn't take the boon carelessly
She patted my back
Cause my voiceless tongue got its essence
finally....

Diving in a Loop

Sitting before the laptop,
Waiting for the screen
To appear on a click
Mind wandered in between
A click would tell
If it was a triumph or a collapse
Hands shook, senses expelled
Eyes stuck on the hourglass
Stream of thoughts waved into the mind
What was it like to be
in a state of capabilities intertwined?
The ideas reframed into a plea.
Countless sleep-deprived nights
Food-habits malfunctioned
Stressful days and doubtful might
Feelings underwent eruption
Pondering, my finger couldn't click
For they lacked the force
The brain echoed with the clock's tick-tick
As the heart was full of unknown remorse.
The cursor pressed, "View"
An error occurred
I wondered if it was a clue
By the universe to reflect, I shattered
The guardian angel dropped a thought in the troubled psyche
What if it happened cause I was not ready?
What if the universe waited for my affirmation?
What if it wanted to prevent me from self-condemnation?
What if all it needed me to believe,
Open my arms to the universe for everything to receive
What if this was the moment of victory?
Thought I, before my laptop, sustaining the mystery.

Somya Nandwani

Somya Nandwani is an 18-year old who's figuring out life one day at a time, just like anybody of you out there! She has fought her battles and conquered her demons, and come a pretty long way till now, progressing each day! She loves to make people happy and aspires to provide them with a safe space to be vulnerable and real. She loves to build genuine connections and live each moment to its fullest potential!

The Uncertainty of What If's

There's too much to do,

There's too much to say,

Yet our egos, image and delusions come in our way.

There's too much to feel,

There's too much to heal,

Yet we remain quiet and seal the deal.

The one you thought is the best,

Yes, he is the one who's carrying a lot on his chest.

The one you thought has everything,

Yes, he is the one whose heart carries nothing.

We are afraid to show our true self,

That's exactly why we search life in a book on the shelf.

Maybe, that's what we were hiding,

Just abiding, never guiding.

I like to talk to people because everyone nourishes a different part of me,

I show them what they want to see, maybe that's how I like it to be.

People deceive, they show the opposite of what they perceive.

But nevertheless, it's what they ultimately receive.

Why is it that we miss it after it's gone,

When our mind wanders and relishes during the breezy dawn?

We feel what even the greatest minds felt,

It's just a little bizarre how skillfully they dealt.

What's the point of feeling insecure,

While facing your fears can actually cure?

Again we depend entirely on our thoughts to reassure.

What is it that you are giving to this earth?

How is it that people shall remember your worth?

At the end of the day it is love that our heart desires,

But too bad this world functions well only for liars.

The Grey Area

The more light I appear, the more deep I am.

The more subtle I seem, the more complex I stand.

I could feel this, I could say that.

I could think no, I could ask so.

I may stand still, I may wanna kill.

I may think why, I may just sigh.

I can be the demon, I can be the child.

I can be the sweetest, I can be the most wild.

I might be dying, I might appear just as fine.

I might wanna get away, I might wanna stay and slay.

I do care, I just don't share.

I do show, I just keep it low.

The more human I appear, the more beast I might be.

It's just what I show you that you see.

The more love I give, the more my hatred shall not let you live.

It's just what I feel, it's exactly what I seal.

The quieter I stand, the louder I am.

The thoughts I express, are the ones I best process.

I rather live the fantasy, I rather ignore the reality.

I rather face the sun, than to face the cruelty.

Coz I am just as human as you are, I'll give you what you deserve, even if it's a scar.

Coz if you take me for granted , your name shall never be chanted.

It's the mind which controls,

It's the mind which decides exactly how our life rolls.

कभी

कभी भीड़ में रहकर भी अकेला लगता है,

तो कभी अकेले रहकर भी एक मेला लगता है।

कभी ज़िन्दगी की सारी ख्वाहिशें जाग उठती है,

तो कभी बहुत मुश्किलों से नींदे टूटती है।

कभी माहौल भरा भरा लगता है,

तो कभी समा मरा मरा लगता है।

कभी किसी की याद आती है,

तो कभी किसी की भूल ही भाती है।

कभी सब कुछ अच्छा लगता है,

तो कभी दुःख ही सच्चा लगता है।

कभी बोलना प्रिय लगता है,

तो कभी चुप होना ही सक्रिय लगता है।

कभी सबका जानना पसंद आता है,

तो कभी किसी का पहचानना भी सर खाता है।

कैसी यह जीवन की माया है,

चारों ओर अनंत छाया है॥

A Farewell To My Second Home: School Life

Yes I am scared,

Scared to let go of the past,

Of the moments that passed by fast,

Cause I know these ones now approaching are some last.

All the learnings I learned,

All the bad ones I burned,

All the success I earned,

All the deep thoughts we shared,

All the feelings we bared,

All the truths we layered,

There's something of everyone that I might keep,

'Cause time is running by taking a leap.

And I know these feelings are going to go deep,

The future may show it's course and do its thing, that is sweep.

Those notebooks, those studies,

Those acquaintances and buddies,

Those walks, those talks,

Those broken chalks,

Where did it all vanish?

Feels like it's been quite a time since banished.

Radhika Dua

Radhika Dua is an educator, writer and speaker by passion. This book is her welcome step into the field of writers. She believes in magic of words that can heal and touch one's heart and soul to the core and wish her words to touch a million soul.

Like it says : जो हो अँधेरा तोह मुस्कुराना ज़रूरी है

हो ज़िंदा अगर तोह ज़िंदा नज़र आना ज़रूरी है

Always and forever!

Always and Forever

One Last Chance

I am lost and I am afraid

I don't know what I want

Searching for paths, I have skipped a lot.

When I started it was clean and tidy

Love was bestowed with promises ready

But, time passed in the running speed

Day by day adding challenges to its greed.

When first time in life I stepped ahead

Life turned me aback

Love is a blessing and I am unblessed

Now again I am exhausted with no passion left

But deep down, my soul whispered quietly

Get ready my captain, let's restart the mission.

Come Back Soon

I was sleeping a sound sleep,

I was with you,

You were with me,

We were all alone.

Deep in my dreams I was holding you close,

It was then that I awoke

With tearing eyes and closing throat,

I Gasped aloud and almost choked,

As if surrounded by clouds of smoke,

The waves cascaded and my heart broke,

I realized that I was all alone,

That it was only me inside my home,

And you were gone for yet another mission.

Though, wait was long and my hopes were strong,

After waiting for long days long

A text received wait for 12 hours or may be more,

My heart ache with grief shaking my core,

Prayers are strong and so our love,

Waiting to hold and hug for long.

I only wished to go back to sleep,

Where we were happily in love and deep

You were with me holding smiles before leaving for the night.

He Still Misses Her

I know that he still misses her

I see it in his eyes and can hear it in his voice,

The girl he met so long ago

That made him feel alive.

I can tell he sometimes thinks of her,

I shouldn't be surprised.

She is young, smart and carefree

He yearns her day and night.

I know he sometimes misses her,

She was passionate to be held

Why wouldn't anyone want her still?

I was under his spell.

But, can he not look deeper

And see my hidden heart,

My needs to please him all day long, have always been on spark.

The distance between us was bruising my own heart

May be sooner or later, he will understand

Why it could never last,

And love like that Is too extreme

It's why she is in the past

I am here right now in front of him,

This love will always last

But, I know that he still misses her

Searching the old her from the past.

My World Of Dreams

I wish I could tear the page

The page of that favorite novel

Step into the world

The world of dreams

Just for once be that little girl.

That girl in the romance novel

Searching the real in the fake world

A prince charming just for me

I wish to be that princess in longing for real Prince,

Or may be that mermaid under the sea.

I wish to escape for just one a day

In a world of fantasy and dreams

Be a part of the adventures and novels that I read.

I could be a heroine

Or may be a witch

A detective solving crimes

Be the villain

Or may be a bitch.

I wish, I could tear the page and step inside

The book that I embrace the most

I wish to find real prince charm

I wish novels were true or may be the characters

I wish to be in his arms and could experience the real warm.

वो वक़्त जो गुज़ारा था

वो वक़्त जो गुज़ारा था

न मेरा था न तुम्हारा था

जीने के कुछ लम्हे थे

हर पल जो बीता हमारा था

याद है वह बैठ के जो

देखा तुमने आँखों में

ठण्ड की किसकी पड़ी थी

आग सी थी साँसों में

वह ठंडी हवाएं

और बियर के कैन

कुछ डांस हमारा

जो भीगे थे नैन

आँगन में बैठे थे

पहाड़ो का नज़ारा था

आसमान था बादलों का

छुपा हर एक तारा था

वो दाल वो सब्ज़ी

वो मैगी वोह चाय

टेढ़े मेढ़े रास्ते

वो जंगल की सराये

इन सभी नज़ारों पे ही तोह

हमने दिल को हारा था

जो लिख सकता था लिख दिया

तुम जानते हो कितना सारा था

वह बीते पल

यौह बैठ के वह रात को

सोचती थी हर बात को

नींद की शायद कमी थी

आँखों में रहती कमी थी

बताती थी हाल दिल अपना

मई बैठ के सुनता था

रात को तोह सो जाता था

दिन में लम्हे चुनता था

दोष उसका न था

दोष मेरा न था

उसका उजाला ना था

मेरा अँधेरा ना था

बताती थी मुझको

अकेलेपन से डरती है

पर साथ रहने से भी कहा ज़िन्दगी सुधरती है

समझाया था उसे

के साथ तोह बस धोखा है

तेरे पास तोह मौका है

वक़्त है अभी तेरे पास

पा ले अपने आप को

सादिया लग जाती है

करते पस्च्याताआप को

यौह बैठ के वह रात को

सोचती थी हर बात को

नींद की शायद कमी थी

आँखों में रहती कमी थी

Jyotika

Jyotika is a graduate of the University of Delhi. She has started her writing journey with Spectrum of Thoughts as a budding writer. She enjoys inking her ideas into words, and she loves artistically expressing herself. She believes in the philosophy of acceptance rather than reaction. She is a happy-go-lucky person and aspires to became an established author.

IN MEDIAS RES

Isn't it a new term? Googled the meaning? Still here?

If yes, let me tell you- **In Medias Res** is a Latin term that means **in the midst of things**. No, this is not created by me, I have learned this while watching a movie i.e. **BROKEN HEART GALLERY**. Although the movie was comedy & romance, where the protagonist's idea of opening a café leads to the confrontation of a hurtful past.

Now, you might be thinking **"How can something be beautiful, when it's broken?"** I guess the broken ones are always the enthralling ones.

Isn't it that the same thing happens with us? When we are in the middle of a challenging situation, someone will always enter in life and boost that lost confidence. This idea makes you believe in yourself more. Like you are important, you are precious, you don't deserve that heartbreak, and you deserve a lot more than what you have been through. In the situations when we are feeling loved there comes a reality check that awards us with pain. Pain is inevitable but what you do with that pain is your choice. Sometimes we can't express what we have experienced, how we gathered our shattered pieces and wore an elegant smile. But there's one thing that tells our story it is **OUR EXPERIENCES.**

We all – in the end – die in medias res. In the middle of many stories!

Happiness: A Journey Or Destination?

Before reading further, just read the title again and answer to yourself, **"Is happiness a journey or destination?"**

Jot down your idea of happiness in your diary/ notes and just read after completing it.

For me, happiness always arrives when I am the reason for the smile on my loved ones' faces or by just helping a stranger. The sparks in their eyes, that mesmerizing smile is the most eye-captivating. Some people find, happiness in expensive things or in planning long terms goals, but my question to them is – Do you have a time machine? I say, when we cannot predict about the next hour or the next second, how can we plan for years? Rather we should learn from the past, live in present, be ready for the future. Also, we should accept the past to live in harmony with the present. It opens space for life's upcoming surprises. Happiness has been like a to and fro in my life. A lot of times I find myself jumping on my feet when someone is happy because of me or even if someone complimented me on how beautiful my smile is. There was a time when it was hard to smile, hard to express myself, at that time I have created happiness either by cooking my favorite dish, or just crafting art, or just converting my thoughts into words. This past year's pandemic made me realize that we need to focus on the journey more than reaching the destination.

"Happy life is a process, not a state of being."

I read this somewhere-

"Either write something worth reading or do something worth writing about".

Isn't it worth it? Either you are creating a masterpiece or someone is creating one for you.

Okay! Honestly writing was never been my cup of tea but this lockdown made me inks those thoughts that were running in my mind. To provide me with this opportunity of being a part of this anthology, I'll always be grateful to my professor for every exposure she provided with all the trust and faith she has shown in me.

I used to be a responsible woman but never an on-stage person, I just used to do the work backstage (honestly I was afraid of facing the crowd), in fact, I never used to write at that time. I started inking my thoughts during the lockdown when I experienced the explosion of emotion, my mind was like a volcano that erupted once left alone with itself, locked in the 4 walls of my home. That was the time where conversion of my thoughts to words started and rescued me from the outburst. I remember during one of the workshops, when I was interacting with one of my coordinators and I expressed to her how this lockdown helped me in inking my thoughts, that time she said, " Jyotika soon, I am going to read something published by you! I trust you and here I am, being a part of this beautiful anthology- **"Self-Talk: Commonly Uncommon"**. The universe has its ways to lighten the path and guide you to whatsoever you desire and attract.

Being a part of this anthology in itself is an indication of universe that it is working out for each one of us and bringing something more beautiful. Universe has its ways and timings; we just need to be patient and open to its magic.

"THE UNIVERSE's imagination is always wider than our imagination"

Tick- Tock! Tick-Tock!

Isn't time the most important teacher of our life?

Well, I know the answer would have been **"YES"** because once in a while in our lives we all have confronted the challenging situation where TIME has showered its magic and tragedies to showcase its importance

"Time changes people, situation & loved ones"

Time has a wonderful way of showing us what matters. It shows the real colors of people in our life. We are the evolved versions of ourselves, every day we become more mature. It's true time doesn't wait for anyone, it just keeps on ticking, and how you utilize that particular time depends on YOU!

With every passing day-month-year, I am turning into a different personality, from introvert to extrovert to ambivert. This pandemic time has given me a reality check and made me question myself - **"Am I alive or just living the life of a robot?"** I am grateful and I hate this pandemic simultaneously, thankful because of my modified personality and hate because of the loss of the backbone of my family. But time has its own ways to teach us the two ultimate truths of our lives: **CHANGE and DEATH,** sometimes they both are hard to accept, they tear us apart but one thing remains constant with time nothing ever lasts. Every morning arrives with a new opportunity, new healing just think of a particular situation from your life where you had thought this is the END, nothing good can happen after this but look here you are, you survived like a warrior. You won that battle of emotions like a warrior. This pandemic made me understand my own self-worth, made me understand the importance of decision making, as one should not regret things later. You should be humble in accepting things as they are but also take responsibility for your life and the decisions that you make.

"Take decision when you have a calm mind, not just to calm your mind"

VIRGO! VIRGO! and VIRGO!

Virgos are exceptions and exceptions are everywhere (the Virgos who are reading this can relate easily). To start cherishing the Virgos let me convey that Virgos are hard to handle. How do I know? Questioning a Virgo, how does she know the traits of a Virgo!

To start with the traits, Virgos are highly demanding, they need the most precious thing from others' end i.e. time and care which is rare to find, also they need the continuous assurance of your presence in their life. They belong to the family of overthinkers. For once try and not answer Virgo's questions and all the possible consequences will already be in the head without any explanation. They prefer to learn about the past of an individual just to know a person better in the present. The song Blank space by Taylor swift clearly depicts a Virgo. They can show you incredible things, from heaven to every sin. They can't bear listening to white lies, if a Virgo asks you to say the truth just do it without a blink because they have amazingly done their work and just want you to accept it without any excuse. They are the ones who never forget the betrayal, they are those people who might forgive you but will never look at your face in their whole life. They observe every minute change in your behavior and then choose their response accordingly, they are never bothered what others will think of them. Virgos are the epitome of perfection and love, they define the meaning of being trustworthy in the real sense. If a Virgo says that you belong to them, they'll turn every stone to bring a smile to your face. Virgos like to talk to everyone but open up to a few, they believe in quality rather than quantity, they are selective. Virgos know how to behave like an open book and make you read any chapter of life that they want you to read. Virgos are hard to find, if you have one, never let go because they'll love you till their last breath. They prefer loyalty, respect, love, and care over physical appearance. Losing a Virgo means losing a person who gave you everything without expecting anything. You are lucky if you have a Virgo, just keep that psycho safe, Virgos are worth it.

BEAUTY OF DARKNESS

Darkness reveals the beauty of life. Night helps you open up to your true self. It's only dark which leads to the light, even our shadow leaves us in the dark. Just think of that time in your life where you were at your lowest point when you don't want to talk to your best friend, irritated by whatever your parents say (relatable?). That's a different phase of our life where the darkness heals our soul and creates its own magic. Nights are the perfect healers, they help you to listen to the inner turbulence and understand yourself better. This pandemic had made me a person who finds peace in the darkness, either it was watching a movie or inking my thoughts, or just reading a book.

Everything that happens in our life is for a reason. Do you know what the good news is? Nothing lasts forever either it is sadness or happiness, it will change from time to time in your life after a time and you will create a place for an evolved version of yourself filled with love and empathy which makes you embrace your flaws with dignity.

The dark phase leaped from my life in August 2021, leading to series of happy moments and times that I can be proud of myself with tears of joy in my eyes. But the lesson that I learnt is beauty resides everywhere in every single thing, you just need to embrace it and never leave the hope just because of a challenging situation, nothing lasts forever. Neither every ending is filled with sorrow nor every beginning is filled with joy , you never know how darkness can bring the light in your life, be accessible and acceptable to every change.

Sumedha

Sumedha Vats is an undergraduate student at Delhi University and has a keen interest in reading and writing. She has done several internships as Content writer. She has a strong desire to express and establish her thoughts and experiences through writing.

Beginning of the end

Samhita raised her hand with a lot of effort (not ONLY because her "aunty" arms were heavy rather because a lot of people were waiting for her to) only to regret instantly as she heard a few chuckles right across her seat.

She tried to be brave at first but then eventually gave up. She looked them into their eyes through her specs and saw a sense of achievement there as what they wanted and she anticipated happened.

She was angry, embarrassed, frustrated but mostly she was ashamed of herself. She hated herself, she just couldn't stand her own self moreover she just wanted to either completely change herself or just cease to exist.

She was trying to act un-affected when the bell rings for the next period. She exhaled anxiety but little did she knew that this period will be even more disastrous than the last one.

Rajendra sir an anorexic, kind off tall social studies teacher flew in the classroom hanging in his regular pale white shirt and a pair of old black pants with ugly shoes.

He isn't Samhita's favourite but still in this time of extreme humiliation and sheer helplessness he looked like an angel to her.

Anyways it was an exciting day for Samhita as that day most of her teachers promised to show the corrected answer sheets for last month's term exams.

She had worked really hard for them and was expecting satisfying results as this was the only domain where she can ace the bullies.

Rajendra sir stood in front of the class with a smirk, he had that typical teacher smirk. All the students were looking at him just like how kids look at their parents when they're going to announce which sibling will be punished more than the other one.

He called out the boys and his favourite ones, the bullies step forward like always.

He ordered "Go to the staffroom and pick up all the answer sheets, they're lying at the left corner of the table."

Viney and Paresh accompanied by Prateek went to the staff room to do the cool kid work. It was high time that Samhita gets the respect that she deserves, and according to her the only way of getting respect was through acing the exams. She wanted to nail every bit of her studies so that she can show everyone who is the real boss. Getting good grades was the only way through which she could gain some confidence to stand with her head held high.

The three "cool" kids entered with the answer sheets and Samhita's heart beat was increasing. This will decide her destiny, this is it, this is the moment she waited for since so long. This is her D-day!!

Rajendra sir started calling out students roll number wise and Samhita was quite later in the list which further multiplied her anxiety. Anyways sir was discussing marks and mistakes of every kid turn wise.

"Roll no. 21!!......Umm Samhita!!" Sir called out in his feeble voice. Samhita got up from her seat and walked as if she is walking down the aisle ignoring all the hushed laughter of the cool kids. They were just about to shut up for life as Samhita was going to get mind-boggling result.

As soon as she reached the teacher's table and saw her marks, she was numb completely blank and then she felt exhausted of it all. She just wanted to smash and scream the hell out of her capacity.

This was her last chance at proving the world that she wasn't just a misfit fat ass here, instead she actually deserves to be here and moreover belongs here.

Now after 7 years later at the age of 19 when Samhita looks back at this incident or rather phase of her life with her current casualties all just seems to make sense.

All she is craving for right now is validation and at the same time is tired by the baggage of expectations. Samhita just wants to shout this out loud so that everyone can listen to her loud and clear:

I'm tired of expectations pouring out of people like hot magma.
I'm tired of my soul expecting me to be someone my loved ones want me to be.
I'm tired of my brain expecting me to be productive all the time.
I'm tired of my heart expecting me to be merry all the time.

I'm tired of my body wanting to be in a specific shape.

I'm tired of my peers being ahead of me all the time.

I'm tired of the society expecting me to fit in somehow.

I'm tired of explaining myself that whatever I did was right for me.

I'm tired of the people around me expecting this world to be a better place.

I'm tired of the expectant eyes looking at me to become something that I can't be and don't want to be.

But the question here is why she is seeking validation, the reason why Samhita was reminiscing the *"good"* old days was to know the answer to this question. And it suddenly strikes her- she is just so weak and vulnerable that she needs someone or something to assure her the worth she carries along with herself.

Good scores are a way of assurance, as they'll give her the topper position along with the constant confirmation from her peers and teachers that she is good, that she is worth it and her existence is valued.

The bullies won't start respecting her no matter if even if she comes first in the whole country, they'll still manage to say "Look how stupid she looks on the stage, stupid cow!!! Why this Buffalo is even being awarded??!!!" hahahahahah.......

Now when she wants people to tell her that she isn't an ugly pig or a fat ass, she just feels pathetic for being so needy. She knows that she isn't ugly and she knows that her worth want dependent on how many calories she takes in a day but still she needed to hear it from someone or anyone for that matter of fact.

The purpose of reminiscing the good old days was partially solved. She got the beginning of her on going end moreover was curious to know the journey from beginning to the end but at the same was exhausted from her own self, she doesn't want to think what's wrong, what happened wrong or what might go wrong?

She wants to shut her chatter box and elude to peace. Thinking of achieving peace gives her a sense of peace but then suddenly someone bangs right into her room screaming "Why are you simply lying down? Just finish the work and sit........." she couldn't or rather didn't wanted to hear further.

Vidya Hariharan

Vidya Hariharan was born in Jamshedpur but her schooling and college was from Chennai. After her M Com, she worked for a few years. After marriage, she moved to Jharkhand and now she is a freelance writer and translator.

I am now in the best phase of my life today! This was my thought as I sat by my balcony overlooking lush green trees of my surroundings. With a cup of tea in my hand I have this surreal feeling inside me which keeps recurring, making me wonder if this is real? I am now blessed with a happy home, where all of us are loving and caring towards each other, I have the most beautiful time at my home with what I loved do as my job and the comfort and independence of financial stability in my life. Looking back, I think was this always like this? No, I feel instantly. But now it seems like that part of my life was ages ago!

After marriage, I have to move to another place like every woman does. With all the pressure expectations of every relationship, time seem to fly away before I could find my footing. I was now a new mother. It was a challenging as well as exhilarating phase of my life. Nurturing my son and managing my family and relations was a bit overwhelming at times though it had many perks like watching a piece of us grow in front of one's own eyes! All the while in the corner of my heart I could also feel guilty of not being able to pursue a job or a career but the pleasure of being able to be with my little one did satiate my guilt to a small extent. My husband Mr. S. Krishnan , an AGM in a public-sector bank, used to go for office early in the morning and come late at night, which left me with no other option but to stay at home to take care of my family. During this time I really had free time to think of what to learn or to pursue my hobbies. After a while I still felt that I could do anything worthwhile while the world around me just moved at a great speed. After marriage I had not pursued my hobbies as I used to before. I love to read a lot of books, write and listen to good music were some of my hobbies. As time flew by , I found I could find some time for myself when my son started going to school. Though I had no clue as to what could be my career then, I came upon a chance offer from a friend to write articles on health and the medicinal uses of various items generally found in our kitchen, for his website. I was sceptical at first, but still wanted to try it out as writing was something I loved. So I jumped into it head on and utilised the time my son went to school to start my work. I had some good reviews for my articles and my friend too was mighty pleased to get well written articles for his website. Along with studies I taught my son to write poems and stories. He was always inclined towards stories and general knowledge about many things just as children usually do. So apart from his school, studies and playing time there was time for us to read books, write and pursue hobbies now. We loved this phase and this went on for a while. My husband had a transferable job and he was transferred to

Chennai. We were happy to come back to our home and I continued my writing job from there too for some days. One day, I got an offer to translate a small book on woman empowerment, which was in English to Tamil. The translation had to be done in 4 days and we had more than 30 pages. This was for a grand event organised for women's day. Completing it within the time was a new challenge for me. I later on came to know that the translated book was well liked too. Both these events gave me a new Avenue to explore and also gave me enough time to concentrate on my son's studies and also take care of my family. My aunt's guide Late Dr. Mithilesh Kumari Mishra, who was Retrd. Director of Bihar education department, was quite close with my aunt Dr. R Kalpana. My mother Dr. Lakshmi kala and me were also well acquainted with her. She was a prolific writer and many of her literary work has been published all over the world. She wrote books in English, Hindi, and Sanskrit, languages and was felicitated with numerous awards all her life. She had been conferred an award by the Thailand's royal family in the year 2013. She wanted us to translate her short stories and poems to Tamil language. So, as a mark of respect to her my mother and I , decided to do it. While my mother translated some of her short stories I translated her poems from Hindi to Tamil. We were invited to Lucknow, U.P to release the book and we're also awarded for or work too. Slowly, many avenues opened for me. The joy of doing creative work and also being able to make a career out of it with the perks of not missing the balance of family care, has made my life not only liveable but worthy and beautiful.

Coming from a family where my maternal grandfather, Late Mr. Ramachandran was a journalist of a well-known newspaper from Patna, my father, Late Mr. A . Hariharan used to write poems too. My mother and my aunt have been freelance translators for a Hindi/English magazine for more than 15 years now, I was always encouraged to write, more so during the time when I was home taking care of my child and family. My son too from very early on in his childhood started writing short stories and poems of which he has a very good collection now. My son, Adwaith Krishnan, is a very good artist too. Inspired by reading books he used to draw pictures of Gods and Goddesses beautifully. My husband, though he couldn't share our family responsibilities with me, has never stopped me from doing things which I liked to do.

As a ray of sunlight that travels through droplets of rain filled clouds and transcends into a beautiful and colourful rainbow, one small opportunity in my life turned it beautiful, colourful and blissful.

Shalini Das

Shalini Das is a life coach and content developer by profession and painter by hobby. She loves to live a life of morals and gives due importance to following values both in personal and professional front. She truly values all the relationships and consider them to be a strength in her journey called life. Other than these she holds a very close-to-heart relation with her baby venture "Creative Think", a training and content writing academy, which has helped her live the life of her dreams.

In My Journey From Expectations to Acceptance

At times nothing looks to be working out, despite everything in place. A happy family life, the world's best set of parents, a caring husband, cute little supportive kids, understanding in-laws, a decent work profile and managed finances, yet every morning we wake up with the feeling that something is not right, something is missing, something needs to be reconsidered, a lack of positivity is direly felt. To add upon, the pandemic had taken a toll over everybody's mind and heart making the situation more helpless.

Has it been happening with all of you too?

Over several months I too have been feeling the same. With the start of the lockdown, physically all of us were caged in our homes. The feeling was somehow different. I felt I have been caged both physically and mentally. I everyday looked at the stacked-up piles of books in my bookshelves that were once my best friends, but now they had a layer of dust on it, with I, not even have touched them for over years. I gazed through my phone finding no songs downloaded though there was once a time when I ran out of storage space on my phone loaded with beautiful numbers, I struggled to find a single individual photo of myself except the passport size photo which I had recently submitted for some official purposes. These made me feel more lost and probably it was the saturation point for me. I realized I was losing my cool and venting it out on wrong places.

I cried to myself, where am I lost. The love and support of every-one around me was not all that I wanted as a help to come out of the situation. Their efforts in helping me to manage the household chores at home made me feel more helpless, failing to realize what was going on within me and why was I not being able to manage it all. Moreover, I could see my near and dear ones losing their cool and patience to deal with the uncertainties of the covid situations and challenges. The one that pained me the most was the anxiety and aggressiveness of my kids, not being able to manage the challenges of the challenging time. I could see my parents and in laws losing hope to live back a normal life again just like the ones we had before Covid-

19 had set in. My husband, whose work had increased manifolds with the new normal of "Work-From-Home" in place, was just too tired to go the same way. Everyone was losing their cool, physical challenges and acnes was taking over our health, kids started being affected with the change in the atmosphere at home. Minor issues tend to take a huge turn. Minor illness was turned to be life threatening in our minds. This really impacted our lives and peace.

My work started being impacted. I realized, I needed to take certain decisions to make things better. But what? Was the big question. Hardly could I fathom out.

I decided to revisit the pages of the books on emotional Intelligence and Neuro Linguistic Programming, that has been a support for me to grow, motivate and put my best in all I did. I started looking for strength and motivation in the pages to help me gain courage to fight the odds and yet manage my cool. The white layer of dirt on the books were quite like one that I had put over my mind and it's time to dust them off. Being a life coach trainer by profession, I started feeling these uncertainties and doubts in mind impacted my training sessions. I felt weak. But probably that was the last set of negative feelings I held back for long. In my journey of rediscovering myself, I chose to learn from my own sessions. I realized all what I trained people to do, I myself was not following.

There started a new journey, a journey that taught me live my life midst the scenario of just passing days in life. I realized it was "positivity" that was slowly fading out of our minds. I started concentrating on work. My baby venture "Creative Think" was quite stagnant since inception. I , till now was randomly working. I realized the importance of clarity and goal setting.

The journey was enriching, and I learned several things, which I now realize are the key for living a life happily. I call it the "Journey from Expectations to Acceptance". I started off slow, with minor changes in my daily routine.

And today, though not fully covered, I feel I have travelled quite a few steps, when at least I am being able to manage myself in a better way. But this indeed was not a simple journey. I took over years to read through my mind and identify what I exactly wanted. This is probably the most challenging question I have ever answered.

Over months I strived to find an answer what I wanted. Though it sounded quite simple, it was typically a difficult journey within my messy mind.

Questions that kept me awake over nights were something in the line like Do I want to go for a full-time job? Or is it flexibility that I want at work? Am I a good mother? Am I justifying my role as a daughter? What stops me in pursuing my dreams? Is it long term benefit or immediate making money should I target? These were just a handful question. No learning is learning unless you can share it as a knowledge to help others utilize the same. In my piece I would take you through how I imbibed the changes and what were the few major changes that I took up during this new journey. Most of them are quite simple to apply and have probably been told to us by our parents and grandparents in the course of our life. But we ignore them.

So come, let's just dive in to set things right all by our own self:

1. Health is Wealth: The fear of visiting a medical facility. The fear of major illnesses. The habit of self- treatment considering all are just minor acnes had been ruling my life. I failed to take care of myself with a proper regime, though I have been asking others at all point to do the same. The increasing pains and health issues, which otherwise looked quite solvable with home remedies, were taking a toll of my mental health. I started overthinking about them and over time developed Nosophobia. Let me call it disease phobia in simple terms. The bad habit of surfing over the pages on internet with the symptoms made me feel like having all possible major illnesses. I started the regime of stopping all self-planned supplements and medications and visit a doctor and take up a thorough health check-up. And thank God all went well. The dilemmas and phobias could get out of my way. This was the first step indeed. The realization that we are good on health and fit to utilize our energy at work is indeed a relief in the time when the world is fighting against all possible sorts of diseases and natural calamities.

2. Self-care and self-love: This would sound to have some selfish intensions. And all our lives we have been told to think of others before we think of ourselves. But believe me, a very true fact is, if we do not love and care for our own selves we can never love and take care of our near and dear ones. Over this while I had engrossed myself so much into the household chores, that I hardly had time to take a few moments out for myself. I missed doing all I had once loved and could not have gone without them. I ignored

my health, and tried to do all household chores by self, feeling that would reduce the workload and physical exertion of all in my family .I am sure, many of you who are reading this too would have done this in some time or the other. This way nor was I able to manage all my chores with perfection, rather I defaulted in completing things in time, moreover I turned exhausted when the day came to an end. Same time, everyone in family seeing me struggling through all these chores started feeling helpless for me. They wanted to extend a helping-hand, but I denied. Though I thought I was helping them by allowing them rest and leisure, I lately realized I were making them dependent and weak, and they were losing confidence in themselves to manage their chores all by themselves. Sitting back with nothing to do, nowhere to go made them rather feel sick. Their health instead of growing better started developing ailments.

Alongside, working round the day, I started losing my cool and vented out my frustration, making the atmosphere in the house quite heated. This promoted bad vibes and made everyone tensed and low.

To get over with all these, I started planning out my days with at least 1 hour for my own self. Though being mother of a toddler and tween I could not get the me time at a stretch but managed to get short spans of 15-20 mins over the day. I started taking up self-developmental courses, planned my daily routine to finish of household chores and responsibilities quite in time. I realized that proper day planning was a must. Though initially I felt I was wasting time, when I was having crunch of time, in planning and writing my plans. But just a few days into following it, things flew smoothly, and I was able to extend to get some 3-4 hours a day to myself. This was indeed an achievement. I took up walks, I started revisiting my hobbies of reading, painting. These not only helped me relax but also I could complete my daily chores in a better way. Not only this, but I also started observing that people around me started investing time for their own hobbies. These transformations slowly helped me get over the feeling of being caged and the aspect of positivity was quite well seen to be hovering in the house.

3. An introspective approach- We have a typical habit of overthinking in a way or other. In any situation, the first set of thoughts in our minds goes to think what the other people in the scene must be thinking, what are his intentions, what made the person take up the, but hardly do we concentrate on how we react or think in a situation and why at all do we need to do all these thinking. This is indeed a big cause of all our " self-created pain". Such thought process, which is among the most common ways we see around us, is the key to negativity in our lives. We need to start concentrating more on what our minds are thinking than the thought and actions of the others, our life would be better and simple.

4. A Gratitude journal-The best self-help tool indeed in a situation, which in our opinion is against our wish, everything seems negative. At a later stage at a later stage, we realize the situation was not that bad like we reacted. Such situations are ample in our day-to-day life and are strong enough to fill up our days with negative thoughts and feelings. Also, such situations cannot be usually avoided. The best way to reduce the down time for ourselves is to manage a gratitude journal and read through it every time we feel low.

5. Unsaid expectations- The unsaid expectations   hold a very important place in creating a negative periphery around us. We have a typical habit of not saying loud and clear of what and how we want things but quietly expect

   our close relations to see and understand it all. At the same time, we are always proud of the fact that we are very strong in understanding the feelings of other, especially the unsaid ones. But have we been told by the other person that we have been doing so very aptly? The answer is a straightforward no. It is just what we feel about ourselves.

6. The magnet mind- The mind works just like a magnet. If you hold good feelings for the person you are addressing, the mind will pull back good vibes. The same applies to your day-to-day conversations and communications with friends, family members and colleagues at work. Try to identify the positive in the extreme adverse situations too and then see a few days of effort bring in a lot of positivity to change the whole atmosphere around you. We

often claim that it's not about me, it is one or the other in the house who is responsible to create the negativity with his/her behavior. But if that one person can make the whole family atmosphere negative, then why not one person with his/her positivity pull in positivity for the whole family. Especially with kids around keeping them cheerful and positive just accounts for some personal time of yours with them and then see the count of positivity over negativity will rule!!!

7. Live in the present- Most of the stress we take up is by thinking what all went wrong in the past and how will we manage the challenges of the future. This makes us stressed out in the "present" and spoils our present. To reflect on the past is fine, but that should be allocated to a specific scheduled time, when we sit for certain planning and not throughout the day. Doing this will make you highly optimistic and help manage depression.

8. Learn to live from children around you- It is rightly said that every person we come across in our lifetime teach us something or the other. This is true even for kids. Believe it or not, children depict an attitude that is usually the best to live a fulfilling life. We unconsciously know and accept it, as I am sure all of us do wish to revisit our own childhood days. A child has a pure soul. They imbibe change very quickly. Also, they can overcome pain and sorrow just in flick of a second. If we as adults can learn to do these, half of our troubles will get over smoothly.

9. Don't mix up your relationships- The habit of comparing people in relationships is the biggest mistake we make. A few common ones are comparing kids with their friends, comparing mother and mother-in-law, husband and a friend, daughter and daughter-in-law and many more. This raises bars of expectations leading to dissatisfaction in relationships.

10. You cannot keep everyone happy- Though I personally try to believe that nothing is impossible, but equally I accept that keeping everyone happy at the same time is "Impossible". "Happy" is subjective term and holds a different meaning for every individual. Hence defining it is not only difficult but quite not possible. We often tend to struggle and suffer in an attempt to make everyone happy. And even if you feel that people around

you all are happy, you will see in effort to make all others happy you yourself are struggling to find your peace.

The above pointers are some practices that helped me in accepting the situation and living it in joy, against continually raising my expectation bar, especially for others around me. The habit of running behind expectations not only reduces the quality of our own lives, but also impacts mindset and health of people around us. Every one of us do face such situations, as discussed above, in some point of life or other. The idea is to get over it with a lower down time. Living by accepting does not mean to live a life of compromise, but rather it is about finding the expectations in what we hold. Though the list of my learnings is long, and I am just half-way in my journey, I felt the easy everyday practices could be of help for someone in a similar situation.

The pointers mentioned above were covered under certain daily habit changes. Let me list it down for your easy access:

- Wake up early. This was the key.
- Spend some "me" time before you run the daily race
- Some meditation or even light music is good to start off
- Maintain a planner. It makes your life easier.
- Don't just eat, for the sake of eating. Enjoy your food.
- Try keeping the gadgets off your hand when sitting for food
- Don't feel shy to ask for rest, if you feel unwell
- Dress up, even at home. You will feel energized and happy
- Pamper yourself. It's a must to survive. Either with some good food of your choice, some good reading or anything that relaxes you.
- Stop complaining to yourself and others. Look within to rectify yourself.
- Comparing relationships make your life complicated.
- Understand and accept that all individuals are different.
- Value people around you. You would definitely discover over your life the value of every relation.
- Write your gratitude journal. Not occasionally but daily. Occasionally can revisit the previous pages to read and relax.
- The last few hours of the day decides how well you can sleep. Try to keep yourself happy.
- Spend time with kids at home or around, they spread positivity.

- Crying does not make you weak. It's a way to release stress. So don't hold back your tears let it flow, if you are upset.
- An incomplete task affects your peace at sleep. Make it a habit to complete before you are off to your bed. Stop reading the minds of others and making wild guesses on who would have thought what, and what were the behind intentions of an act. Better keep a track of your mind and fill it with the positive side of every situation.

I understand the list is long and difficult to manages. But to start with you can choose a handful and slowly grow to take over more and more of these as part of your daily routine. The day you are able to make at least some 10 of these a habit, you can proudly say to have covered a long way "From Expectations to Acceptance".

As a life coach, in my journey of coaching over 500 adolescents and adults, especially housewives and mothers of young kids, I could well relate my situation with theirs when they speak about it. As an effort to extend my contribution towards many with whom I could not connect one-on-one, I took up the attempt to pen down my learnings. Even if one person can bring in some change in his/her life following these regular practices, I feel my effort would be rewarded. I bow my head before those, who smile with a heavy baggage of responsibilities on their head, that does not allow them to choose a life of their choice and dreams. But I am sure, Self-love is something they can try upon too, as that does not cost much time or means. Also, at the same time I am sure there are many who have the required support and means for a comfortable life but have been clueless of what they want and have been leading a life full of stress and dissatisfaction. Such a situation is just because we kept expecting and hardly did anything to express gratitude that what we have is something many do not have. We can give 100 reasons to ourselves for not being able to manage the above said practices, but if we try to give one reason to choose at least one of these practices, I feel we can make our lives better.

I am a dreamer, and all my life I have been dreaming a life of king size. Not in terms of money, but in terms of happiness. I am sure you too must have dreamt it once. So, what are you waiting for? Try out the learnings to "Live Life King Size".

Dhyana Buch

Dhyana Buch is studying in class 10 IG. She loves music and creating music. Her hobbies are playing guitar, badminton, reading and above all travelling

Dear (despised) Coronavirus

I am writing this letter to inform that you have rattled our world with your presence! This global pandemic caused by you has disrupted the lives of every person living in this world. I miss going out with my friends to watch movies, I miss being at school arguing about issues and debating about stupid topics with my friends (we could still do it, but it would feel much better face-to-face). I miss traveling to different places, trying out new restaurants and cafès'. But, I guess you should not be blamed for we are responsible for this ourselves.

Our world has been overpopulating since the past few years and it has become a global issue, China had its "One Child Policy" which was quite foolish of them if you ask me but since you're not let me get back to what I was saying. In my perspective, it was nature's way of restoring balance in the world. This quarantine has given me a lot of opportunities to focus on my interests like blogging, vocalizing, singing, and also trying out new recipes to learn how to cook! It made me see things a bit differently, I mean, people were so obsessed over having an image in the society, having a perfect body, going out to click "candid" pictures, and just doing stuff that never made sense to me. You would have to "maintain an image" or you would get the "last cup of coffee" in the meeting(Gilmore girls reference), which is a very dreadful thing in the society.

I admit that things were getting a bit crazy and busy for me at school, more than I'd like to admit, but this impetuous getaway type of break has given me a lot of time to focus on my blogging and doing things that I wouldn't ever get time for with the craziness of being in the first year of high school! So, don't go feeling too precious or of being royalty in our world for that matter, because you're not. Many people have actually benefited from you and found a new perspective in life, something which they couldn't while running around in their offices 24/7.

All I'm trying to say is, I am very thankful for this time off, but I miss the outdoors a lot. I am used to traveling to different places for my summer vacation, which now I'll have to spend confined in my room. Go visit some other planet, Corona. Cause you are already running around in workplaces, spreading yourself, just like people run around, promoting themselves. I think you should learn from our mistakes and go on a vacation to Mars or Pluto, Afterall, you never know. You might return being the cure instead of a disease.

Yours lovingly hated,

Just Someone Honest

Those places are all I need

I was on my seat 26F,
with the most beautiful view
The feeling too familiar
I loved the feeling of a plane taking off
Carrying me away to faraway lands
I still remember the way I held her hand on my first flight
She assured me, "There's nothing for you to worry about"
Going back to that moment I remember gazing out over the night sky
Imagining myself touching those clouds
As if I could feel them
Caressing my hands and wrapping me into a bear hug
Which should have been warm
But they weren't
They were cold and icy
And suddenly I remembered
I was still inside the plane
I started laughing at my absurd nature when I was 5
The pilot spoke over the inter phone, "We are now nearing the beautiful city
of Paris,
The city of love. As we can see the signature monument
On your right..."
My eyes travelled towards the window and right out
It was heavenly to see La tour Eiffel
Outside an airplane
At such a close proximity
My heart started beating heavily against my chest
It was so so beautiful
Never could someone describe the scene in words
More perfect than the picture itself
Nostalgia captured me to the times when I had
Visited Singapore only to have a look at Merlion
And my! He was absolutely stunning
The beautiful sculpture stopped me right in my tracks
Also the time when I visited Switzerland
And I could swear right at that moment
No place could ever measure up to Interlaken
But each time
Each trip that I take to a new land

I learnt that all those places were beautiful
In their own way
In their own perspective
If only people would look at the world with a different angle
These places could also include people as
A factor of their beauty,
They say live life the way you want
I think
Tu ne peux pas vivre assez, si tu n'as pas vu assez

How To Get Motivated To Be Proactive

This morning, I woke up and realized... what will I do today?! I have been spending a lot of time writing lately, so whenever I take a break, I start watching Netflix or listen to some music. I know that it is not enough, so, I tried out some new techniques to get myself motivated and encouraged to learn and create!

5 Basic Steps To Get Motivated>

1. Plan Out Your Goals
- We all want to achieve something in life. To start somewhere, note down your goals on a parchment, your laptop, or any device and book. I have written my goals in places that I visit the most. I keep at least 10-12 reminders on my devices that remind me of my goals every week. This helps to organize our interests and builds a thinking process.

2. B - Positive!
- Sometimes looking at the brighter side motivates people to not give up on their goals. Optimize your options, ponder upon them. I have my room full of motivational posters, quotes, favourite bands, and artists, etc. that help me feel at ease. If all the famous artists, speakers, politicians had their life worked out, so will ours... Be Positive about the things you feel you won't ever be able to achieve.

3. The Pen Is Mightier Than The Internet :P
- Well, the internet is obviously mightier but writing on paper can help a lot too. I have this small journal where I write down my dreams, aspirations, goals for the month/year and I keep slashing them off whenever I've achieved them. There is this powerful feeling that you get when you slash off that item off of your list, and suddenly you feel like you want to get all the things done!

4. Baby Steps... :D
- We all know that no one has ever had it easy on the way to achievement. I know, I know, some of you might be thinking," It's my freaking vacation! Why should I plan out stuff right now? I've got plenty of time, right?" WRONG. People never have enough time to get things done and from the way I see it, life is a pretty long path. There will be new goals, new perspectives, and new aspirations. So the goals you set now and the goals you will set then, are interdependent. Start with 10 minutes of writing your

goals, then 20, then 30, and soon all those minutes will count up to slashing those items off of your list! (I have no idea how I got this wise :P)

5. Get that Partner-In-Crime!
- I know that my friends have always been there to support me, encourage me to take up new opportunities and they've had my back since as long as I can remember. I've taken up origami and art because of one of my friends who is great at drawing stuff and sketching. Find that person who is willing to take all those steps with you to your destination. Sometimes we need a push and no one better than a good friend can do that.

All these steps have helped me through the past few years and I hope they help you too. Every single teenager right now would literally be binge-watching on Netflix, cooking something or being bored and staring at the ceiling. This post was inspired by my new "Quarantine" routine that I've made some adjustments to so that I can get enough time to have fun, study a bit, and learn something new!

"Creativity doesn't wait for that perfect moment."

Stay Safe and Stay Healthy!
Adios Amigos :D

Nilesh Sangtani

Nilesh Sangtani a.k.a Nilu Baba has been composing poems since very long time but did not believe his poems would ever get printed with other great writers. He is a business man by profession, a designer by hobby, a motorcycle rider by passion and a poet by nature. He believes in HOPE-Helping Other People Every day.

Ride

एक नया एहसास हर बार होता है

जब मैं अपनी बाइक पे होता हूँ

कुछ अलग ही मेरा अन्दाज़ होता है

जब मैं अपनी बाइक पे होता हूँ

लोग मुझे जाने या न जाने

मेरी पहचान तो खुद से ही है

जब मैं अपनी बाइक पे होता हूँ

जीत जा

जीत जाना एक दिन मुझको है

पल पल मार्क जीना अब मुझको है

न जाने दूंगा इस चीज़ को अपने से दूर

जीत जाने की हिम्मत अब मुझको है

ये दुनिया भले कुछ भी कहे मुझे

मेरा दिल बस हर दम चाहे तुझे

करता रहूँगा बस तुझको मैं प्यार

हर दम करता रहूँ बस तेरा दीदार

बारिश

ए बारिश की बूँदें

मुझे अपना बना लेना

दिल करता है तुमसे रोज़ मिलूँ

मुझे रोज़ बुला लेना

खुश हो जाता हूँ एक छोटे बच्चे की तरह

फिर रो पड़ता हूँ एक बड़े आदमी की तरह

कभी निकलने को बाहर मेरे कदम झूम उठते थे

आज सरपट अंदर दौड़ता हूँ एक चूहे की तरह

मैं आदमी हूँ, ये भूल गया था

मेरी शिकायतें बहुत हैं

ये भूल गया था

मैंने तुझको गर्मी भागने को बुलाया था

अब भीगने से घबराता हूँ

एक बिल्ली की तरह

ए बारिश की बूँदें

मुझे अपना बना लेना

दिल करता है तुमसे रोज़ मिलू

मुझे रोज़ बुला लेना

मिलने की देरी है

मन की बात आने को है जुबां तक

बस मिलने की देरी है

आँखें बोल देंगी सब कुछ

बस मिलने की देरी है

हाथ मिलके सब हो जायेगा बयान

बस मिलने की देरी है

फिर कुछ कहना न होगा ज़रूरी

बस मिलने की देरी है

एक नज़र ही काफी हो जाएगी

बस मिलने की देरी है

वक़्त काट जायेगा

दूरी मिट जाएगी

फांसले होंगे काम

बस मिलने की देरी है

सफर

ये मंज़िलें

ये रास्ते

ये दूरियां

ये सफर

बस पालक झपकते ही

जाएगा ये गुज़र

इन रास्तों में कुछ तो है

खींचा चला आता हु मैं यहाँ

ये दूरियां अब दूर नहीं लगती

सफर ये लगता है सुहाना

पल पल यहाँ बिताने का मन करता है

ढून्ढ लिया है, यहाँ आने का मैंने बहाना

होनी थी

करलो बात

उनसे जिनसे

होनी थी न हो पायी

एक मुलाक़ात

उनसे जिनसे

होनी थी न हो पायी

साँसों की डोर बड़ी कच्ची है

देखो टूट न जाए

उनसे जिनसे

जुड़नी थी न जुड़ पायी

क्या कहुँ

तुझसे हमेशा डरता हूँ

क्या कहुँ

तुझको हर बार टालना चाहता हूँ

क्या कहुँ

बाहर मिलोगे या घर में कहीं

इंतज़ार नहीं, बस तुम्हारी खबर रखता हूँ

क्या कहुँ

सब कहते हैं कितना ज़िंदा दिल हूँ मैं

सबको अपनी पलकों पर बिठा के रखता हूँ

क्या कहुँ

तुझसे मिलना तो होगा एक न एक दिन

मिलकर फिर वापस नहीं आऊंगा

जानता हूँ

क्या कहुँ

ए मौत तू आनी थी

अब आ गई है

लेजा कहीं ऐसी जगह

जहां मरकर भी सबसे जुड़ा रहूँ

अब और कैसे कहुँ

तू ही है

एक रिश्ता बनके तेरे सामने आ गया

एक एहसास बनके तेरे दिल पे छा गया

तू ही है, वह तू ही है

एक झलक ही काफी थी तुझे अपना बना लिया

एक पुकार ही काफी थी तेरा दामन चुरा लिया

तू ही है, वह तू ही है

एक दोस्त बनके तेरा रहना चाहता हूँ

एक बंधन को ज़िन्दगी भर निभाना चाहता हूँ

तू ही है, वह तू ही है

एक अरसा बीत गया उस पहली नज़र के लिए

एक जनम और ले सकता हूँ उस पहली नज़र के लिए

तू ही है बस

तू ही है

Unnati Chandwani

Unnati Chandwani is a story telling writer and a dress designer from Kanpur. Her words are her own experience of life piled up to make a beautiful verse. Her love for travelling and music give serenity to her life. She wishes to fly high with the power of her imaginations.

Single Child

My love of life

You are my only child,

Don't have two or three

But you are the one in my destiny

I know you are single

Always wanted someone to giggle

Your pain for sibling

Always haunted in my brain

Your heart filled with loneliness

When you see kinsfolk nearby

Things are not always of our choice

But few are in possession of life

But I promise to hold you on

Never let you feel alone

Try to sing and play in your zone

To make you gladsome all the day long

You are not only my single child

But also my true sunshine

Hey Girl!

Hey girl, don't be so shy, get up

And learn to say no or goodbye

You don't owe to a girl or guy

You are enough for the joy

No need of society's toy

Hey girl don't be so shy

Get up and learn to give a try

Don't tag yourself with perfection

For the sake of other's satisfaction

Hey girl, don't be so shy

Get up and learn to leave a lie

Don't be so fool to live with

Who always make you cry

Hey girl, don't be so low or high

Get up, comply your dream and fly

Don't let your fright halt to touch you sky

Hey girl, never ever be shy

Learn to say word of your justify

School Life

Those were the days when I was happy
With number of pencils and erasers by my side

Those were the days when
Teachers were my threat
But still their small appreciation
Was my greatest asset

Those were the days when
Appetite was on height
Still parathas and pickle blended with
Maa ka pyar was my fancy diet
Those were the days when
Friendship day was my biggest popularity check
Friends were just for colourful hand strap

Those were the days when
Sudden rain holiday was my delight
It was my veneration which make me bright

Those were the days when
Smile was pure not fake for sure

Those were the days which
Are treasure of my heart
Whom no one can take apart

इंतज़ार

है सलामती के जहाँ का

खुशियों के आसमान का

इंतज़ार है उन फ़िज़ाओं का जो मिटा दे

दर्द ज़हरीली हवाओं का

अब और नहीं देखना मंज़र जलती चिताओं का

इंतज़ार है उस बागबान का

जहाँ फिर से हो जाये इंसान इंसान के नाम का

अब और नहीं देखना खौफ हर दिशाओं का

इंतज़ार है ऐसी हवाओं का

जहाँ असर हो जाये सबकी दुआओं का

अब और नहीं देखना आलम बेबसी का

टूटे हुए ख्वाब और गुम सी हंसी का

अब बस ख़त्म हो इंतज़ार अपनों के दीदार का

नया सा गुलिस्तां हो बस प्यार ही प्यार का

माँ

माँ तुझे लिखूँ तो क्या लिखूँ

तुझमें पूरी कायनात समाई है

मेरे वजूद में मैं कहाँ हूँ

तू ही तो मेरी परछाई है

मेरे बचपन ने तेरी लोरियों की कहानियाँ सुनाई हैं

तेरे आँचल की छाँव में धूप सुनहरी समाई है

माँ मेरी कामयाबी तेरी ही दुआओं ने सजाई है

भूल गयी तू अपने ख़्वाबों को

रख दिया छुपा के उन किताबों को

उम्र भर बिखेरती रही होंठों पर सबके मुस्कान

एक पल भी न सोचा दफन करते हुए अपने हर अरमान

क्यों सिमट कर रह गयी घर की दहलीज़ पर तेरी पहचान

माँ अब तेरा हमसाया मुझे ही बनना है

हर कदम पर साथ तेरे चलना है

हर ख्वाब तेरा मुक़्मल करना है

तेरी उन दबी सी आरज़ुओं को फिर हकीकत करना है

माँ अब तेरे वजूद की नयी दास्तान लिखना है

Hitika Awtani

Hitika Awtani is a student and has immense interest in story-telling and writing. She is 13 years old, with hobbies like playing sports, watching television and practicing art and craft. She attempts to encourage people, particularly teenagers, to fight against unnecessary bullies smartly.

Email: hitika.awtani16@gmail.com

Things I Tell Myself

Hi! This is me Hitika! I am writing about confidence. Basically, me being a victim of bullying will be giving advice to you guys who might feel low and sometimes lonely.

There are a lot of people who are teased for their looks, body, their way of talking, etc. The only quote I will tell myself is 'Love Yourself'. If you don't love yourself, then who will? You are beautiful.

Be ready to give answers to people who are jealous of you. For me that word 'jealousy' is the only reason they tease you.

Make-Up

This word is the worst. Why would you ever want to cover your own beautiful face. Pimples, acne, black heads, fat, double chin, all of this is ok! You do not need to contour for the perfect jawline. Yes! Taking care of your skin is primary, but don't use the beauty blender to touch up your face. Even I have pimples, acne and blackheads, and I am ok with it.

Your hair, let them breathe. They don't need heat to be straight or curly. Even my hair are super curly and hard to manage but I will not put any chemicals on them just for them to be straight.

Attitude

My vibe is nature and self-love. some more quotes I tell myself are- Winning and losing isn't everything. Sometimes the journey is just as important as the outcome. One reminder- If you really got a pure heart, just know you are going to win in the end. Ok?

Keep loving, the world needs more love.

Also another daily reminder- when you are putting yourself together, it will get lonely. Choose growth over someone's company, every single time and always remember why you started. Never give up on yourself.

Every time your friends won't be there to support and encourage you. You are the only one who will be with you three sixty-five days, twenty four hours.

Weight/Size

My main motivational speech- I am fat. Not an insult or compliment, simply a statement of fact. I have some flab, but I don't look crap. In fact, I look fab. But I am fat, nonetheless. And please don't make this a contest of who's fatter or thinner. We all deserve dinner. We all look like winners, some of us just happen to be fat. So being fat is ok!

Take all the comments as compliments as the people do tease but this does not define who you are, it shows who they are. All that matters, is you being yourself.

Social Anxiety

The fear of being socially judged is one of the most common forms of insecurities. Like I mentioned before, people who judge are perhaps jealous or scared of you. Don't let them get in your head or brainwash you.

They will try to put you into down and steal your spotlight, but you don't let them be successful. You are much stronger than what they think.

I know I have been repeating this phrase but at the end of the day, you have to love yourself. You have to be independent and take risks to live your life.

You live once, so live it at your fullest!

Not Being Worthy

All these physical insecurities represent one mental insecurity that is really the root of all evil, i.e. not being enough.

Sadly, our world thinks that good looks are everything. It does not matter what people think, what only matters is your opinion.

Think positive! You are beautiful! You are unique! You are perfect just the way you are!

Perfectionism

No one is perfect in this world. Everyone has difficulties in their life in some or the other way, shape or form.

You don't need fame, make up, money or anything to be perfect. Actors aren't perfect either. You should wake up with a smile on the face and sleep with a smile. Be happy for what you have. Loving your family, yourself and your friends is the most important thing.

Conclusion

The only way you will be able to succeed is by ignoring people's statements. Be your own guru, leader and bodyguard. Try to forget your past and move on. Stop talking to people who demotivate you. Don't ever have blind trust on anyone. Be ready to face your fears, regardless of how you feel inside.

Also, Marie Curie once said, " Life is not easy for us".

We must have perseverance, and above all, confidence in ourselves. We must believe that we are gifted with something and this thing, at whatever cost, must be attained.

Bhumika Parmar

Bhumika Parmar is currently studying in 10th standard. She started filling colours of writing in eighth standard. Through her poetries she has tried to express the colours of love and affection.

An Uncommon Perspective Towards Common Things

Ocean

I am measured in fathoms,

Deep blue with the rippling n gurgling sounds,

I am calm n serene

But when in fury

Can bring havoc n destruction on the planet.

Marine life, aquatic animals, sea food

Are my treasured attraction.

Who am I?

Sea ocean sagar or samudra

Love

Love is an unconditional feeling, expressed in many ways.
Your gestures speak of love.

The soothing caress of a mother for a child is love.
The care and concern of a father is love which has no words but expressed everyday unconditionally.
Siblings love each other since childhood, their bonding is inseparable since they are toddlers. They express this by bullying or by teasing each other.

Passion for anything under the sky is also love expressed beautifully be it dance, painting or music.

Its boundless vast sometimes mystic but very blissful and giving.

Happiness

Happiness is a subjective thing felt differently
Watering the plants to being a shopaholic to family hangouts
And the list goes on.
All adds to your happiness.
Inner peace is the only way to be happy always.
Now a days next human is materialistic
As they crave for monetary gains but are not happy.
Happiness can be found in little things,
The graph of happiness increases everyday
Through simple and trivial things
Simplicity is the key to happiness

Mother

Sun rises in the east and
Sets In west but mothers
Love never sets.
It rises beyond the directions discovered

She is my alarm
My bestie,
My teacher,
My mentor

Coz in all ways she is the best
I don't criticize other mothers
But I just love my mom the most

She teaches me to chase my dreams
And work for them not just daydream.

I love her from the bottom of my heart
Coz in all ways she is the best.

She scolds me hard and loves me the hardest
Coz in all ways she is the best.

Ring

I'm precious
I'm adorned by a lady
I must be there in an engagement ceremony
Or the occasion would be incomplete...
Any guesses?
I am a Ring...
Round, oval, triangle or square
Any size any shape
I beautify a finger and fit perfectly

Gold, silver, platinum n imitation
I'm made by innumerable metals
Studded with gems, ruby pearl and much more

I'm a gift of joy forever

Nature

Stars shine bright in the sky
But we don't have time to see it from our sight

Waves ripple all day through
But we don't like to hear them through

Leaves rustle and create a sound
But humans are nowhere found

The pitter-patter of rain is all in vain
As time flies we can't wait

And that is what I hate!

My Father

Someone asked me that who is the person
Who will love you unconditionally
My answer was my father.

The hero of my life.
That hero who doesn't require makeup to shine
The hero who doesn't need to show his biceps.
He is my hero my father.

My best friend who will always keep my secrets safe.
He is my partner in every prank I play .
He always cheers me up when I am down.
He is the best person I ever found

From walking to talking he taught me every thing
The teacher of my life to whom I will be always a small princess
My father.

THE END

For contacting publication, VISIT:

Website:- www.sotpublication.com

Instagram:- https://www.instagram.com/spectrum.of.thoughts/

Linkedin:- https://www.linkedin.com/company/spectrum-of-thoughts

Twitter:- https://twitter.com/spectrumpublish